JUST LIKE ME

MIRIAM SCHLEIN
Illustrated by MARILYN JANOVITZ

HYPERION PAPERBACKS FOR CHILDREN
NEW YORK

Printed in Singapore.
For more information address
Hyperion Books for Children, 114 Fifth Avenue,
New York, New York 10011.

First Hyperion Paperback edition: April 1995
1 3 5 7 9 10 8 6 4 2

Library of Congress Cataloging-in-Publication Data
Schlein, Miriam.
Just like me/Miriam Schlein; illustrated by Marilyn Janovitz.
p.   cm.
Summary: A mother rabbit tells baby rabbit a story about a rabbit's
adventure in the wild, and it turns out to be a story about him.
ISBN 1-56282-233-0 (trade) — ISBN 1-56282-234-9 (lib. bdg.) — ISBN 0-7868-1037-8 (pbk.)
[1. Rabbits — Fiction. 2. Mothers and sons — Fiction.
3. Storytelling — Fiction.] I. Janovitz, Marilyn, ill. II. Title.
PZ7.S347Ju   1992
[E] — dc20   91-40019   CIP   AC

The artwork for each picture is prepared in ink and watercolors.
This book is set in 20-point Garamond Light.

To Teasel
—*M. J.*

"Tell me a story,"
said little cottontail rabbit.
He was brown, with a white belly,
and he curled up close to his mother
in their little round nest in the meadow.

"All right," said his mother.

"Once," she said, "in a nest in a meadow,
there lived a little cottontail rabbit.
He was no bigger than a little wild sunflower."

"Just like me," said the little one.

"Now, this little rabbit," said his mother,
"was a great jumper.
Sometimes, when he jumped,
it seemed to him he could take off like a bird,
and fly away, over the mountain.
That is how high *he* jumped."

"Just like me!" said the little one.

"Now, one day," said the mother,
"it happened that this came true.
The little rabbit jumped.
He jumped so high,
and he jumped so fast,
that there he was,
up in the sky like a bird.
The wind was behind him.
It pushed him along.
And soon the little rabbit found
he had really jumped right over the mountain.

"Then, he began to fall.
Down, down, down he came.
He had no wings to hold him up,
so down, down he came."

Little cottontail, there in the nest,
squeezed his eyes shut tight.

"But it was all right," said his mother.
"The little rabbit landed soft in a leafy tree."

"Oh," said little cottontail.
"He didn't get hurt?"

"No," said the mother rabbit.
"He didn't get hurt.
He was a lucky little rabbit,
as well as being a high jumper.

"He hopped quickly down, all safe and sound.
Then he ate a lot of the sweet grass and clover
that was growing all around."

"He sounds just like me,"
said the real little rabbit,
giving a lick with his little pink tongue.
"Are you sure the story's not about me?"

"Oh no," said his mother.
"It's not about you.

"Then," she said, "he heard a noise.
What could it be?
A mink? A skunk?
He did not know.
So he froze to a stillness,
there in the tall green grass."

"Freeze!" said the real little rabbit.
He lay so still, he did not even breathe.

"But it turned out to be only the wind,"
said his mother,
"blowing through the grass
and making it rustle."

"Whew," said the real little rabbit
there in the nest.
He began to breathe again.

"So," said his mother, "that little rabbit
that flew over the mountain
shook his ears, then went on his way.
He hopped zigzag
through a field of wildflowers.
Then he took a sunbath.

"Now, after a while,
a big black cloud blew in front of the sun.
It got all dark.
That little rabbit looked around.
He was ready to go back home,
back to that little nest,
all lined with his mother's fur.

"He looked up at the tall
mountain he had jumped over.
It was rocky and high.
He tried to jump it,
but now he could not.
The wind was blowing the wrong way.
He tried once.
He tried twice.
He jumped way, way up.
But the wind kept pushing him back."

"Oh," said the little one,
sticking his head into his mother's fur.

"Being a high jumper was not enough.
Being lucky wasn't enough, either.
But he was a smart little rabbit as well,"
said the mother rabbit.
"If he could not jump back over the mountain again,
he knew what he could do.
So he set out, right then and there,
and hop-hop-hopped *around* the mountain.
It was a long trip.
His paws got tired.
But finally, he was home."

"Just like me,"
said the little one, lifting his head.
"Because here I am!"

"Yes," said his mother.
"And when that little wandering rabbit
came hop-hop-hopping home,
his mother was so glad to see him."

"Just like you?" asked the little rabbit,
blinking up at his mother.

"Yes," said his mother...

"Just like me!"